Zoren
Child of God

Sarah Duffy

DEDICATION

This book is dedicated to my children.

CONTENTS

ACKNOWLEDGMENTS

Thank you, Yeshua HaMashiach, for Your glorious light; otherwise, I would be lost

1

Roots

An old woman sat in a chair with one of her small grandchildren in a dim room with a crackling fire whispering in the corner, two other children huddled under blankets as the wind howled outside.

"Tell us a story, Gigia." one said.

"Yes, please tell us a story, Gigia." said another child.

The Grandmother said softly, "I only know one story, but it is a great story. It is our story."

~~~~~~

Not long ago the whole world was covered with darkness, but God the creator of the entire universe sent his only Son into the world laying down His life to destroy the darkness that ruled the land with an iron fist. Jesus was crucified and resurrected and His blood poured out for all sin. All authority was given unto Him and His name lifted above all names. Before Jesus Christ ascended to the right hand of Father God, He charged His disciples to go into all the earth and spread the good news of redemption from the evil one, so that all people would come back into right standing with God.

The gospel of Jesus Christ burned brightly piercing the darkness with a deadly blow as the light of the Holy Spirit was carried one by one and swept the earth like a wild fire.

This was the beginning of the church and soon the first of the apostles passed their mantle to the next generation of those who studied under them, and they passed the responsibility to their students until every village had heard of Jesus Christ our Redeemer and Lord. Families were being brought into salvation; wives were bringing husbands, sons bringing parents, friends bringing friends, grandmothers telling their grandchildren until entire villages were being added to the church every day.

One such village was Makarios, a small fishing village full of hearty, industrious laborers. They were good hearted, generous people; in fact, Makarios means blessed. The Gospel came one day by storm and transformed the entire population.

One marked by God for salvation was Andrian. He was a peaceful man truly blessed with a big family. Andrian had a talent for fixing anything and he never turned anyone away because they could not pay. He consistently told his daughters that good always returns to a giving heart. He loved his wife and they had nine daughters, but no son. Andrian longed for a son and God heard the secret prayer of his heart.
Andrian had plenty to share and welcomed the traveling apostles Caius and Alvita into his home at every opportunity. When they visited Makarios, they were drawn by the holy spirit to a busy cove where many people bustled and toiled. There they saw Andrian entrenched in work mending fishing nets.

Caius and Alvita were a husband and wife who worked together as a team to bring the message of salvation throughout the region. Alvita, moved strongly in prophecy. Filled with holy spirit she spoke confidently of God raising up leaders out of unlikely places to overcome all the familiar strongholds that destroy legacies and cause generations to be cut off.

She prophesied to Andrian, father of nine daughters, of a grandson to be born to his family that would be used of God. This seed of his heritage would lead an entire kingdom of people into salvation and back into covenant with Christ through his bloodline.

Twenty years later that prophesy was beginning to be fulfilled when Zoren was born to his mother Amira, the tenth daughter of Andrian of Makarios.

2

Zoren

Inside each and every one of us are treasures from God waiting to be unlocked. All it takes is belief, and the faith to stand in the power of God's Spirit. The Spirit awakens within each of us the keys to our true heritage in the spiritual kingdom.

All things have been made available to us, God's children, by the greatest act of love by Jesus; that He would give His life for us. We have been forgiven of all sin and the barrier of unrighteousness has been removed by the blood of Jesus Christ, the only begotten of God.   Jesus was born for this very purpose, to trade His perfect life for ours, and to die a painful and humiliating death, so that all people could be made new, and available to be used of God through Jesus' atoning blood. We can only truly know God, and we can only understand who we were created to be in Christ by the Holy Spirit. Our true identity in God's Kingdom is waiting to be revealed and this knowledge awakened in each of us by the Holy Spirit alone.

God has a plan for each of us laid in the foundation of the earth and it is up to us to search it out.

Zoren could never know what great things lay before him, because his physical eyes could not perceive all the activity around him in the spiritual realm. As with Zoren, so it is with us. The spiritual realm, although mostly invisible, is more active and more alive than the earthly, physical realm. Many can even pretend the spirit realm doesn't exist...in fact; they are unable to see it, virtually blind, for spiritual sight is only activated and accessed through the Holy Spirit.

Each one who desires to see in the spirit realm must only ask God. Through prayer, spiritual sight and understanding will be opened. Simply ask all things in Jesus' name and Jesus said it shall be done. Receive by faith and see the truth.

Spiritual perception is so important. It allows one to not only see the schemes of darkness, but to see what God's angels are doing. One will see His good plans to advance the kingdom of heaven. It allows one to become adept and to recognize opportunities to do God's perfect will on earth and to make more sound choices.

Zoren, a little boy and Amira, herself a widow, knew she could never raise him to fulfill his great purpose without God's spiritual help. This led Amira even closer to the Lord Jesus through unceasing prayer. Amira instructed Zoren to pray daily,

 "Father God in Heaven, here we are kneeling before your throne. We come before you as your children. Open our eyes to understand your spiritual truths. We receive them now in faith. Amen."

  As ordinary and quiet as it felt at times, Zoren was never alone. He prayed to his heavenly father all the time -- whether he was gathering sticks in the forest, or pulling weeds in the garden, or feeding chickens, or skipping rocks. Zoren could always talk to God.

Zoren had one play mate, his cousin Ziyanna, she was born the same night as Zoren and they shared everything together. Zoren protected her and watched her very closely. Never were there two children more closely bonded than these two cousins.

Zoren's natural father, Renn, was swept away at sea during a sudden storm before Zoren was born. Renn had fled his country Ragost and his crown and found refuge with the christian church. There he journeyed with men of God to Makarios to serve, where he made a life far removed from the pagan kingdom of his birth.

Renn loved Amira and desired to protect and shelter her from his past. Renn's father was the mighty King Shaan of the pagan land Ragost. He was an ancient idolater whose entire land was cursed and blood thirsty, with demon powers enchanting men's hearts. There every evil thing they thought of they did with no remorse or restraint.

The safety and harmony Amira and Zoren felt in their close-knit family was about to end as King Shaan's soldiers closed in on their village. Shaan searched for Zoren in order to take him as his heir and dedicate the child to Shemhuth. Shaan believed Zoren, being a male, belonged to him. The evil king would do anything to snatch Zoren away from his mother and their Christianity.

The kingdom of Ragost with Shaan the ruler at its head employed the priests of Shemhuth. There they built grand temples in Shemhuth's honor and poured blood on those alters for power and greed. So dark was this kingdom that even the queen, Brigitta, fled for her life into the mountains with her coven of sister witches, for Shemhuth had no mercy and he demanded complete subservience. Brigitta would never submit to any man or demon.

3

Taken

The Soldiers of Ragost had come and waited for the right time to strike, and attacked the women. One soldier struck Amira on the head and left her unconscious, taking Zoren from his bed in the night.
 As Amira slept her dreams took her to a mountain top. She heard the rocks crying out like a thousand small voices calling out to her in urgency. The very foundation of the earth rumbled and groaned as if every soul felt a sharp pain. Suddenly, an angel's face appeared before her. Like
translucent molten metal it glowed and sternly commanded, "Wake up!"

Amira jolted and sat up in bed stunned as she began to recall what had happened. An eerie feeling washed over her. There was a low ringing sound that sent her nerves into a panic as she quickly recollected the horror. Amira's body exploded with pain from all the spiritual flags alerting her. It sent pins and needles to her limbs and gnawed at her guts. The hair on her neck stood on end. Her heart sank and she gasped, it felt like she was dying! The air she breathed in felt so heavy.

Amira tried to call out but nothing came, no sound. Silently Amira prayed, *Lord! I need your strength!* She made her way to Zoren's room but he was not there. He was gone! It had happened. They had taken her son and Amira was living her nightmare.

She wanted to talk, in fact to scream but all that would come out was a guttural, muffled moan straight from the center of her soul. She feared the worst and the thought of her son lost forever sent imploding pain to her middle. She crumbled to her knees. Shortly she spotted Ziyanna in the corner. She appeared unharmed. Amira raced to her and scooped her up. She was so thankful for Ziyanna!

Amira tried to speak, tried to ask Ziyanna if she was hurt, but only a gurgle came out. Tears soaked her face as she embraced Ziyanna. Sounds began to come out of Amira's mouth. Her tongue moved but she could not understand this language she spoke! She cried out and tried to say 'Jesus' but she could not make her brain and mouth work together. The only sound she made was this heavenly language that poured out of her soul like liquid flames. Out of her mouth the flames shot into the air and an opening appeared through which angels swooped one by one into the room and touched all the wounded sisters, who began to stir.

 Amira felt like she would burst. Finally words came.

She screamed, "FATHER! I need you! My son was taken! I know you love Zoren more than I could, and I know all things are possible for you. I can only find him by your power!"

 "Amira!" A voice loudly proclaimed.

 "Here I am!" she answered.

 The room flooded with light for a moment. Three angels stood in front of Amira and a silent Ziyanna. Amira squinted her red, swollen eyes. She averted her face, she was too empty to feel afraid and she knew she needed this help from God.

The Angel that spoke was very tall. He towered over Amira. He looked like a man but his complexion gleamed. He spoke, "I will take you to your son." The power of his voice overwhelmed her senses and sent a tremble through her body. Her bones shook within her. She felt the marrow of her bones fill with warmth, and her heart felt a tremendous peace as love poured into her.

A giant light entered the room. The force of it blew her hair back! Out of the light came a long red cloth that shimmered and sparkled as if the surface was alive and moving, while at the same time thick and soft. An angel that stood back received it into his hands. The angel said, "Amira, all your sisters are accounted for. We have healed them and they have taken the girl to safety."

He reached out towards her for her hand. Amira closed her eyes. She felt a blast of air then she felt her body go weightless. She dared not look. In a flash they were in the dark. The atmosphere had changed. It was cold and damp.

They were in a hidden cave reserved for rituals to honor the pagan god Shemhuth, the god of power and destruction. Pagan priests were huddled in a circle, cleaning and wrapping up the tools and knives they had used during the ritual performed. The king had just offered Zoren to Shemhuth in a dedication ceremony of bloodletting in an attempt to tie Zoren to this god and to give these demonic powers control of his heir.

Amira gasped and tried to hide herself. The angel that had been speaking to her previously said, "They cannot see you. We are cloaked from the physical realm. We may move freely, but disturb nothing of these pagans."

Amira spotted the alter. Her face paled, blood felt as if it left her body. Her stomach twisted and it took all her strength to hold back the urge to vomit. It felt as if her soul burst apart and everything in her blew away into oblivion! The loudest, pain filled scream could never do justice to the feeling of utter depletion in that moment.

   Amira raced to Zoren. He was bound
tightly and blindfolded with a black cloth. He
was not coherent and she was somewhat
glad for that. Unsure of what to do next, she
awkwardly pawed her fingers, she breathed,
and she was not sure when or if she had
been breathing. She saw breath coming
from Zoren and she knew he was alive so she
could breathe.

The angel who had received the cloth came and touched Amira. His strength bathed her skin. She absorbed power into her flesh and it washed over her. Amira's thoughts began to collect and order themselves. She wanted to get Zoren out of there quickly.

The angel handed the cloth of righteousness to her and she wrapped Zoren in it. It was as soft as the finest, spotless lamb's fleece. It was gorgeous to touch and healing power emanated from it. The cloth was very long and it wrapped around Zoren many times. It covered him completely and made him invisible in the physical realm as well.

The cloth was brilliant red. No color like it to compare it to, it shimmered and danced. It seemed to live and breathe. Only the angels could hear and understand, but the cloth sang out in a soft soprano, "Mercy, mercy, mercy."

Two angels placed their hands on Amira and Zoren. They began to glow brightly and blur. Then in a flash the party disappeared.

4

The Throne

A soft light faded in and Amira clutched her son. She moved the cloth from over his face, then removed the blindfold and threw it away with contempt. Soft breezes moved around them as the scenery began to come into focus. The breeze blew tiny beads of laughter around them. The oxygen was full of fragrances and exotic flavors she had never experienced before. There was an overwhelming peace, a completeness of soul that stilled her. She knew absolutely what was true and there was no hesitation in her thoughts.

She stepped out and noticed the texture she stood on had a spongy texture. It was not quite solid but she stood upon it. She looked down and it was an endless sea, perfectly still and undisturbed, though it sparkled and glistened like the oceans she had known before. They seemed to be in a giant hall that had no enclosures but the space was confined by invisible waves of power that were stronger than walls of stone; however, beings were walking through them all around.

Amira could feel her body being absorbed into this thick atmosphere where everything seemed to flow together. Everything silently communicated in a unified frequency and all things behaved as if each part were connected to one another in a liquid form. Amira's emotions melted into the fold and mixed together with an overwhelming sensation of joy that seemed to resound off of everything in beautiful sound waves.

Suddenly, everyone and everything turned and took notice of an immense light drawing over the place. It filled the entire grand hall. It was a perfect sunrise and burned brightly as it approached rapidly. It exuded a strong peace that took over one's mind and took captive every negative thought and surrendered it to an undeniable truth. This enormous light was larger than eyes could perceive and it was the most beautiful image. It stirred tears in the human heart. The light came off and cleaved to everything it approached. Amira fell to her knees and wept for how beautiful the light was.

A man's form came out of the light with His eyes shown full of love. It was the most loving face Amira had ever seen, and she knew it was her Lord Jesus. Jesus reached out and touched her and her body flooded with an intense love. A texture of warm oil poured over her and enveloped her.

Jesus spoke gently but every word pierced through the atmosphere with authority. "Amira", He said, "the sound of your tears touch my heart." Jesus took Zoren into His arms and kissed Zoren's forehead. His skin began to glitter and sparkle with gold.

Jesus scanned Zoren. With just a thought the leather bindings around Zoren evaporated. Jesus peered into Zoren's chest and reached in to pull out long, black thorns from Zoren's soul. One by one Jesus pulled out the thorns. He spoke to the thorns and commanded them to "Burn!" As He did they burst into flames and disappeared.

Jesus reached into His gleaming coat and retrieved a gold key. It fit perfectly into Zoren's heart! He turned the key and as He spoke golden words came out of His breath, dancing onto the air. The words had a powerful energy and glowed brightly like glowing embers. They went into Zoren's chest and he began to glow. The words landed on Zoren's heart and made soft, doughy impressions that turned to gold and glimmered.

Jesus said, "This is the Word of God spoken over Zoren. This is who he is, his future and every scripture that he needs to know to journey through his life and bring his mission for God to fruition." Then with His finger Jesus signed His name on Zoren's chest and said, "You are found spotless and blameless before Me."

Jesus turned to Amira and handed Zoren to her. He called forward two angels with broad wings. The angels approached, holding a beautiful garment in their hands. The garment was of the purest white, made of fine linen. It had been sewn with gold thread all along the border and the entire fabric was embroidered with gold writing.

Jesus gestured to the angels with a nod and they placed the garment over Amira's shoulders. The embroidered words of gold began to speak and to tell Amira of her victory! They went on to tell all the names of her grandchildren and her great grandchildren and of the many triumphs and victories in her path.

Catching her eye, Jesus said, "You are never alone and I hear you when you call out to me. You are a good and faithful servant! You will always have a home and a shelter in me."

A sound erupted, trumpets blasted, and a loud voice said,
"Only trust in my Spirit! He is always speaking, always speaking what is true. You must learn to lean into the Spirit I have given you. Only walk when you are in my Spirit! Everything must be taken captive and forced to align with the Holy Spirit.

Jesus continued, "For the Spirit of God has fruit so that you can know it is from Me. The Spirit is always producing and His fruit is always love, joy, peace, patience, kindness, goodness, gentleness, faithfulness and control of your flesh. Your enemy cannot deceive you when you walk in this knowledge and he cannot overtake you or cause you to stumble."

As if a giant, seven-story curtain had been pulled back, in front of them appeared a huge mountain of glistening purple amethyst. It was so huge that it towered over them like a massive castle! In the shadow cast over them was a knee crippling power that roared over their bodies.

Zoren's eyes opened and he looked around puzzled. Amira fell to her knees, buckling in the awesome presence of God. Zoren looked down at the glass sea they sat on. Under him he saw fish swimming deep below. He pressed his hand into the surface and it molded to his shape. Zoren pierced his hand down into the water and drew up a handful. It felt like water but it did not behave like water. The drops all pulled together like a stable structure.

Two angels bowed, took their assignments and disappeared in a gentle burst of light. Next, two angels swooped Amira and Zoren up in their wings and flew them up to the throne of God. They landed and placed the two of them into the palm of the Father's hand. The Throne of God was massive and it seemed to never start or end. His hand was metallic and had every color imaginable in it. The surface had no color and every color all at once. God's love for His children, His people, is so strong that in His presence a word does not need to be uttered. The truth is just known and felt and understood.

Suddenly they were back on earth, back on the road that forked. One way was home to Makarios. The other way was out into the great unknown, leading towards the great journey of life to be fulfilled.

5

The Path of Light

Zoren was a thin boy. His stature was not what one would think of as a warrior of God; a warrior to lead and transform a kingdom. However, a believer's power does not come from his physical attributes - it comes from within one's own spirit. In the submission of one's Spirit to Jesus lies the power to overcome every power of darkness and heal every trace of its destruction.

   Zoren's eyes twinkled like the sea as his mind soared into dreams and visions of all he had encountered in the throne room. He tried to comfort his mother as they were about to part and go separate ways. Amira was to go home to Makarios and Zoren was to find the path of his destiny, not alone but with the Holy Spirit and with the Word etched into his heart, and with Jesus near and angels all around.

"Mama, everything you ever told me has prepared me for today," Zoren said as he took hold of the edge of her cloak and looked up into her eyes. "I am ready... and I am not alone."

Amira smiled softly, holding in tears and choking back a well of emotion. *It doesn't seem to make this any easier* she thought. Amira tenderly kissed her son and released him to go. "I love you, and I will pray night and day for your swift return."

Zoren, not knowing exactly what to do, prayed out of his heart. "Father, Your word is the light to my feet and a lamp to my path."

The ground rumbled gently and the grass dried up, revealing a path. Stones of light emerged from the dirt and shone with heaven-like brilliance into the dimming sky. Dotting out into the distance the path made its way forward and the stones emerged ever so far off in the distance. Zoren could see the starry twinkle of the lit up stones. Trees and bushes scurried out of the way pulling their veiling foliage from the clearing of the path, leaving a large visible opening for Zoren to travel unobstructed.

With a deep breath Zoren took his first step into the future to face what he may, knowing God had sent angels, and they were watching him as he walked away from home and on the path of light. His mother Amira watched and prayed as he shrank out of view. *A person can never know how much they love*, she thought, *until they have to give it all to God*

The Lord of Darkness, the god and master of Shemhuth, had sent evil scouts to watch Zoren and to try to stop him from completing his journey. The two spies did everything they could to place traps and snares under leaves and brush to lure Zoren to step into them. They travelled ahead and dug pits with sharp spikes in the bottom for Zoren to fall into, but the prayers of Amira strengthened the alertness of the angels with Zoren and gave them the authority to stop the plots of the scouts. As Zoren approached a pit or a snare, the ground would speak to the angel and the angel would tell the path to swallow the trap and with a clap the earth would close and the path settle.

In the dark Zoren began to feel alone and he began to shiver. Heaviness sank over him and he heard a sleazy sneer, "All alone in the dark little boy?" The light of the stones seemed to dwindle in a haze of darkness and Zoren's heart began to beat with fear. Zoren couldn't see anything but he heard the voice again. It snickered arrogantly, and in a wicked game it said, "What, you can't see me? That's because I'm in your head!" The voice roared with laughter at its own cleverness and said, "Run, Zoren! Run if you can!"

The path began to close in and claw branches began to spring up in front of Zoren as his pace accelerated, scraping and scratching at him. He felt as if he was being chased by wild beasts. The Spirit of Fear mercilessly pursued Zoren. An odor spread like a mist around Zoren and it overwhelmed his senses. His head spun in a panic.

Out of nowhere leaves and vines crawled out of the ground like a pit of snakes and grew up in bounds, enveloping the path and choking out the light. Zoren was encapsulated all around in a jungle of thicket shooting up to the sky. Rapidly the branches and leaves consumed all the empty space and little, sheer, piercing thorns grew out of every crippling twig. Zoren could not go around, under or over, nor even very near. The twigs seemed to jump out, grasping at him and trying to gash his skin.

Walled in on all sides, Zoren had nowhere to go but into the maze of darkness before him. The walls were so high he could only see their towering span, not knowing where or even if they ended, or if they went straight up to the edge of the atmosphere. The sharp thorns made it impossible to touch or climb the branches and the vines seemed to drip with a black poison.

Zoren was frightened, breathed heavily and his heart pounded. It hurt to even draw a breath. His limbs trembled at the thought of being trapped in the dark. Zoren took off running, but the further he ran, the path twisted and turned and closed in behind him, as if it were a phantom chasing him in the woods.

Zoren saw what he thought was an opening only for it to close up swiftly as he approached it. It was a cruel game of "keep-away" this demon of fear played. Frustrated, Zoren fell down and grabbed at the dirt. His eyes welled up as he looked up towards the sky, and whispered, "Even the darkest, deepest pit cannot separate me from God."

Zoren touched his heart with his hand. From the very depths of his heart, he felt a word come up from under his hand and into his mind. The Word said, "Nor height, nor depth, nor any other creature, shall be able to separate us from the love of God, which is in Christ Jesus our Lord."

Zoren prayed, "Father, I am lost and afraid! Help me in Jesus' name. I cannot do this without you." Zoren paused, patiently listening. A tiny twinkle appeared near Zoren. It began to move faster and swarmed as it multiplied into thousands of living golden fireflies. These lights danced and encircled Zoren like a cloud of galactic lights.

Zoren jumped to his feet. He reached out to touch the strange substance and like a flash flood the Holy Spirit overflowed inside of him! He felt his belly combust with holy fire. It did not hurt but he could feel flames flickering on the inside of him. Zoren was being anointed with warrior zeal and power from God! He was being equipped.

The tiny lights began covering and coating his clothing. The lights attached to his arms and hardened into shining armor of light, and etched in gold with the Word of God! From above descended a bowl full of scarlet that cried, "Mercy!" It morphed before Zoren's eyes into a helmet of pure white metal. As the helmet slowly fit itself to his head he heard an angel proclaim, "For a helmet wear salvation!" Zoren's heart responded, *Believe in Jesus and you will be saved*!

The light covered Zoren's chest like a strong hug. The little light beings bonded together and in a flash of light, the strongest white armor fit Zoren perfectly. The angel spoke again, "The body armor of Righteousness!" A belt swirled around Zoren, resting at his waist and fastened snugly. "Gird yourself in truth!" the angel said.

"Walk in peace!" As the Angel said this, steel boots materialized over Zoren's shoes. The light swirled and rested on the boots coating them in white and inscribing God's Word.

"Here is your shield of faith to extinguish the fiery darts of the evil one," the angel declared. Lights moved around, then a shield as big as Zoren appeared in the air. It gleamed and the tiny lights inscribed it with gold as he took hold of it in his left hand.

Zoren said, "Where is my sword?" as he stuck out his open palm to receive it.

The Holy Spirit responded, "Open your mouth Zoren."
Zoren obeyed and as he opened his mouth, a shout of victory came out! He exclaimed, "God did not give me a spirit of fear, but of love, power and a sound mind!"

A giant three-foot sword abruptly shot into existence. It was sharp and glinted as light dashed from its blade.   It was massive and looked like it would be too heavy to wield; however, as Zoren took hold of the handle he found that the sword was light and effortlessly moved as it cut through the air.

"Thank you God! Thank you for your armor and might!" Zoren lifted his thankful heart to God, and as he did the blade of Zoren's sword burst into flame!
The spirit of Fear who had been hiding and observing from a distance let out a gasp.

Angels of God appeared all around, some of them singing the praises of God. There was a resounding buzz of heavenly language all around and the sound began to rise. The earth began to rumble and one by one the trees and the bushes and brambles imploded and fell upon themselves and burst into flames. The entire maze disintegrated into a million tiny particles and blew away.

Zoren stood tall with his sword ready. He spoke to the spirit of Fear, "In the name of Jesus, I command you to leave. I am covered in the salvation of Jesus Christ! You have no authority here. Leave this place and never return!"

Zoren's words ripped through the demon. It shrieked, began to spin and was pulled up and away like it was trapped in a whirlwind until it was out of sight. A few lesser demons ran away after Fear yelping like small frightened dogs.

6

Iohanan

It was quiet now. Peace was restored and the stones of light had reappeared. They popped up out of the ground one by one. The night was beautiful and the moon shone brightly over Zoren as he ventured down the path again. The stars above seemed to serenade softly like a choir of light in the heavens.

"Angel?" Zoren said, not expecting a response. He looked over and saw a ten foot tall angel towering over him.

"Which one of us do you mean?" said the angel and motioned his hand in a circular gesture.

One by one the army of angels made themselves visible to Zoren.

Shocked by this, Zoren tried to recover.

"How come I can't see you all the time?" asked Zoren, trying to sound at ease. Zoren looked up at the angel, squinting his eyes at the light bouncing off the angel's bright face. Zoren moved his hand to his brow to shield his eyes, as he tried to see the angel's face more clearly.

The angel did not answer. He folded his arms and stood like a strong, stoic guard. He had a thin face. The bridge of his nose curved sharply and he had long, wavy, golden blonde hair that rustled in the wind. This angel looked more disheveled than the others Zoren had encountered in heaven. He had a solemn look with his lips tightly pursed. He did not seem to like talking.

Zoren was glad to meet him and was glad that he could see the angel. "May I ask your name, Sir?"

"Iohanan," he stated frankly. That was the last thing he said when the path suddenly ended.

They stood side by side in awkward silence until Iohanan faded out of sight, though Zoren could sense that he lingered nearby.

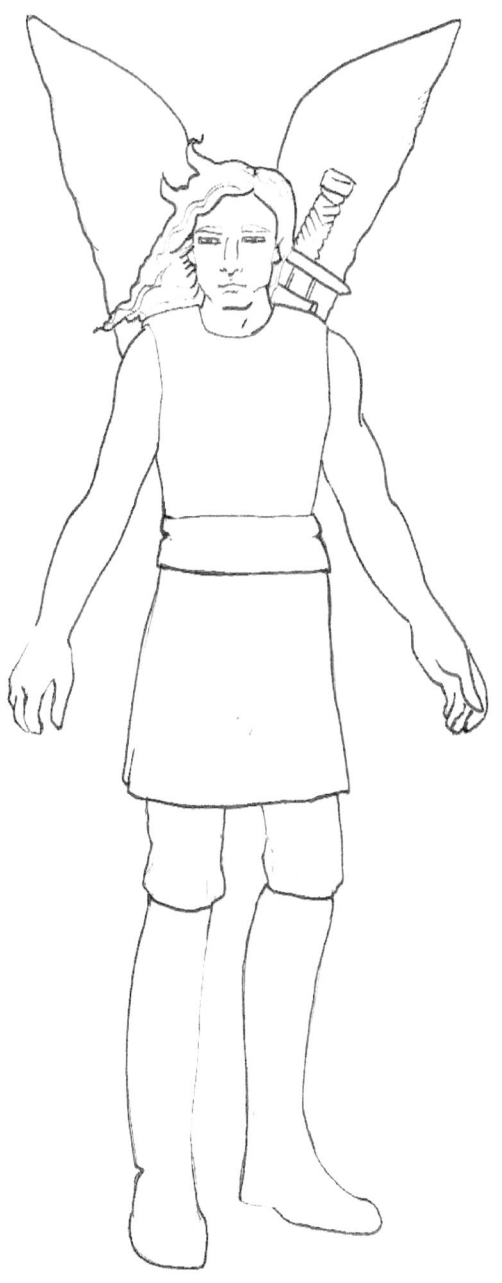

Every day one must choose if they will run and hide or stand and fight. The evil darkness that presently fills the earth would have us run and hide but God want to empower us through his Son Jesus Christ to stand and fight.

As dawn began to break, the path of stones dimmed and began to dry up and turn into mist. As Zoren reached the end, before him was a cliff peering out over a valley. In the midst he saw the castle cut from black stone, with its towering peaks piercing the sky like dragon talons. Zoren knew this was his destiny and this was the next challenge he would face. He would go in his armor of God, sealed in Jesus Christ and confront the enemy face to face.

~~~~~~

The old woman, Gigia, looked around at her sleeping grandchildren; she gently tucked them in and kissed their foreheads. The little one stirred as Gigia tugged at the blanket that had slipped off. "Gigia, what happens to Zoren?", "Tomorrow." Gigia smiled, "I'll tell you, tomorrow." The little one closed her eyes and drifted off into her dreams of the great adventures that awaited.....

Zoren

ABOUT THE SERIES

Sarah wrote about Zoren to represent a person who felt counted out, a person who had lost before they even had a chance to begin. Zoren represents the person that no one believes in. But God uses these types of people to confound those who think themselves wise; those that believe they are powerful are actually weak. For strength is only from knowing how to grasp onto the hem of the wing of the one true King. It is those that believe in God's power and rely on it so completely those are the ones useful to God. You just have to want it more than anything else.

www.ingramcontent.com/pod-product-compliance
Lightning Source LLC
Chambersburg PA
CBHW021940170626
46807CB00007B/3204